2023

For Jax ♡

May the Lord bless and

keep you always ♡

In His Love,

Jodie ♡

# REX and MATILDA

Jodi and Pierre

ISBN 978-1-0980-2254-9 (paperback)
ISBN 978-1-64416-950-6 (hardcover)
ISBN 978-1-64416-949-0 (digital)

Christian Faith Publishing, Inc.
832 Park Avenue
Meadville, PA 16335
www.christianfaithpublishing.com

Printed in the United States of America

# This Book Belongs To

_____

# Introduction

This is the story of Rex. Well, it's actually the story of Rex and Matilda, just like the title says. Rex's mom told him that when he was born, she and his dad decided that this was the perfect name for him. She told him it meant "king," and since he was such a big strong baby, it just seemed right. Ever since he was very young, Rex was always the most curious and most brave of all his friends. And Rex always felt like he was the biggest and strongest in all the land...at least in his heart.

Rex lived with his mom and dad and his little sister, Matilda, in an arroyo behind a row of houses in the desert. The desert was an interesting kind of place to live. At first glance, you never saw too much of anything going on—but if you were very patient and looked really close, so much was always happening! Of course, there were lizards, but there were many other creatures in his neighborhood as well.

At the break of each new day, there were mourning doves that would wake him with their cooing. There were quail and woodpeckers, scorpions, spiders and snakes, jackrabbits and field mice, and even javelinas and coyotes. There were agaves, prickly pears, sage bushes, and organ pipes. There were even the giants of the desert—the saguaros. And the flowers! There were so many flowers, all so bright and beautiful!

Rex loved where he lived because there was always a new friend to be made and somewhere new to explore. And when he got tired from all his exploring, he loved to find a big warm rock to lie on. He would just bask in the sun with his family and friends, lazily soaking up the sun's warm rays. When it got too hot, there was always some cool dirt under a stone or a shady leaf deep inside the sage bush to relax on. As night fell, he would always be tucked safely in and listen to the hooting of the local owls. As far as Rex was concerned, this was the best place on earth.

Rex and Matilda were not only brother and sister, they were also the best of friends. Every morning after a delicious breakfast, they would scamper off to find something new to investigate. Rex always made sure to keep an eye on his little sister. Whenever Matilda was a little afraid to try something new, she could always count on Rex to help her through. One time, when they were climbing to the top of the highest saguaro around, Matilda became more than a little afraid. Halfway up, she froze—she couldn't go up or down. She just froze. She was really starting to panic, but then Rex stood up at the very top and yelled out, "I'm Rex, king of the desert! I will rescue you, my fair lady!" Then he curled his arms to make his muscles really big (at least as big as a gecko could) and growled loudly. Matilda laughed so hard that she almost fell. Then she scrambled up as fast as she could and gave Rex a great big hug. She loved

Rex so very much, and he always seemed to make her feel safe and happy.

And even though Matilda was the little sister, she was always there for Rex when it seemed like nobody else was. Sometimes, when they would be out playing with their friends, Rex would start going on and on about how he was the biggest and strongest of them all. He would go on and on about how he could climb the highest or run the fastest or lift the most. Needless to say, most of the time his friends would just laugh at him. This would make Rex feel so very sad. It's not like he wanted to brag so much and always be the best, he was just born that way. Why couldn't they just take him seriously once in a while?

Matilda knew that her brother had a big heart, and even though he got a little full of himself sometimes, she knew he meant well. She never failed to stand up for him when his friends would laugh. "Yeah, you just go ahead and giggle," she would say. "One day, my brother is going to show you all just how special he really is!" Then the two would head home together. They would always be quiet for a few minutes, but then Matilda would make sure to seek out a big bug or listen for a strange noise. She would cry out, "Rex, I'm afraid!" And he would forget all about his feelings being hurt and comfort her with a big hug. He loved his little sister so much—he knew that she did these things on purpose. He knew she did them to make him feel better, and it always worked. He really loved being her big brother.

One day while they were out exploring, Rex was doing a lot of thinking. For some reason, the usual stuff they were doing just seemed boring. This didn't happen very often. After all, he truly did think this was the best place on earth. But sometimes—just sometimes, he felt like there was something more out there. Whenever he got this feeling from time to time, it always made him feel restless. Rex decided that this was the day he was going to do something about it.

Nearby, there was a park with a fantastic playground, just past the boulders and across the road from some houses. It was just on the edge of the arroyo. On this particular day, Rex looked at Matilda and said, "Hey sis, let's go over to see what those children are doing."

Matilda's eyes widened. "Oh no, Rex!" she said. "You know I don't like to go that far!"

"Well, we don't have to go too far," he explained. "Just close enough to get a better look. Besides, those kids are always having so much fun! Don't you want to know why they're always laughing?" Now Rex had Matilda's curiosity going, and before they knew it, they were inching their way to the park. As they were making their way to the playground, Rex's heart was racing! He had always dreamed of making friends with the children. Even though they were so very big, something about them was different from the other people he would see go by. Now, finally, he was going to see what all the excitement was about!

When they got really close, they climbed safely into a sage bush and peered out from behind the leaves. What Rex and Matilda saw was beyond anything they had imagined. There were children everywhere! They were climbing on giant beams that seemed like the hollowed out cacti they knew, only these were shiny silver in color and tangled in the craziest way. They were sliding down the smoothest hill, and some boys and girls were even holding on to big long vines and flying through the air at the fastest speeds! Some of them were riding on the wildest animals Rex and Matilda had ever seen!

While they were watching in amazement, Rex and Matilda became aware of something else as well. Even though they had heard the children laughing from far off, the laughter never sounded as sweet as it did now. These voices were the happiest sounds they had ever heard. Rex and Matilda looked at each other and made a promise—this would be the first of many trips to visit the children. Just before dinnertime, they scurried home as fast as they could. On their way, they made another promise that this new place would be their very special place from now on.

Before too long, visiting the children became their favorite part of every day. Just being around them made Rex and Matilda so happy. It was that very happiness that made them more and more comfortable at the playground. So comfortable in fact that one day, they didn't even notice the boy, kneeling down behind them to get a closer look. The minute Rex saw his smile, he knew they were going to be friends. Matilda, on the other hand, was not so sure. Rex stood as proud as he could and readied himself. The boy reached down and softly touched the top of Rex's head. "Hello, little fellow!" he said. And with the kindest look they had ever seen on any child's face, the boy gently scooped Rex and Matilda up in his hands. As Matilda felt the warmth of the boy's touch, even she knew that they were safe. Rex and Matilda huddled tightly as they went higher and higher, moving closer and closer to the boy's face – so close they could even feel his breath. In silence and wonder, they all gazed at each other for a little while. Then the boy said, "Well I'd better put you down right where I found you." And just as gently as he had brought them high into the air, he placed them back in the exact same spot on the rock.

From that day on, Rex and Matilda looked for the boy among all the other children. When they would spot him, the two would watch his every move and talk about that exciting day when they met Peter. They knew his name was Peter because every day his mom would stand outside a nearby house and call, "Peter, time to come in now!" He would lift his head with a great big smile and call out loudly, "I'm on my way, Mom!" And their special boy would run home as fast as he could. Yes, they did consider Peter their special boy. Rex and Matilda decided that this was because no matter what Peter was doing, he was always ready to share a little kindness. Even if he was playing, he offered a helping hand whenever needed. Each time he went sliding, he patiently waited his turn. If he was climbing, he was always so careful and never got too rough. One time, when he was swinging, a smaller child fell and began to cry. Before anyone else even noticed, Peter ran over to help. The little child was smiling in no time. No matter what Peter was doing, he seemed to care about everyone around him. For these reasons, Rex and Matilda had a very special place in their heart for him.

From time to time, Peter would stop by the rock, looking for his tiny new friends. If he spotted them, he would always give them a big smile and a gentle pat on their heads. Sometimes, he would even bring a small piece of fruit for them to enjoy. Peter was kind of happy that the other children never seemed to notice. After all, his new friends were so very small, and to Peter, time spent with Rex and Matilda was a very special treat.

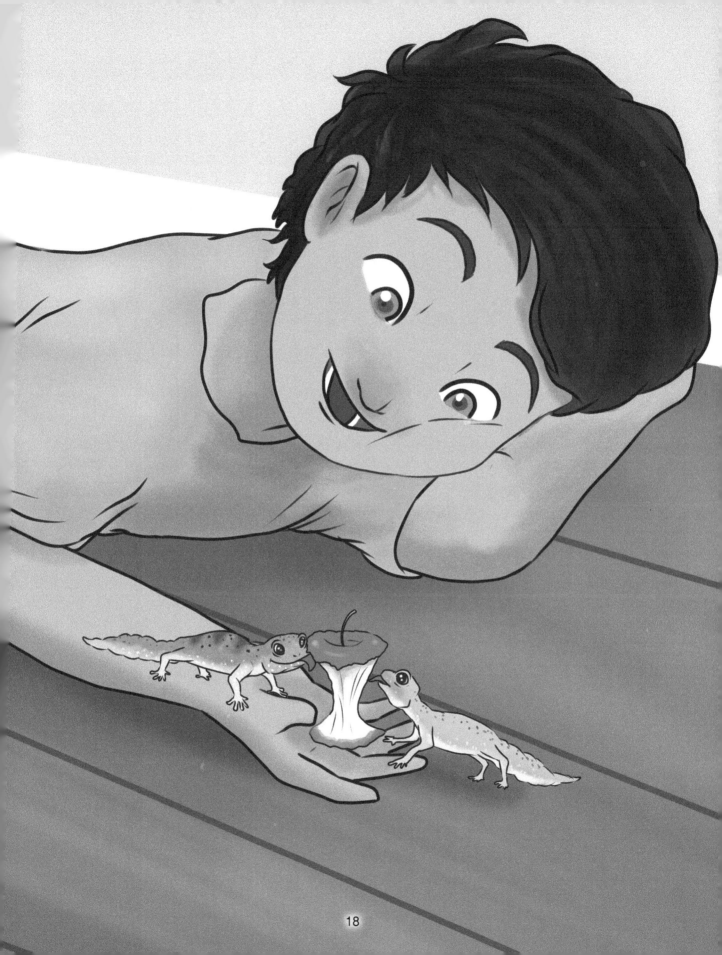

One afternoon, Rex said to Matilda, "Let's follow Peter today and see his home up close." Matilda thought it was a great idea! Soon Peter ran off. Rex and Matilda did their best to keep up. By the time they reached the door, Peter had already gone inside, so they scurried up the side of the house and peered into the window. Right there in front of them was Peter's family—smiling, talking, and getting ready to have dinner. As Rex's belly growled and he thought about his own delicious dinner waiting for him at home, Peter and his family did something Rex and Matilda never saw anyone do before. Even though all that yummy food in front of them was just waiting to be eaten, the family didn't touch it. Instead, they gently held hands, closed their eyes, and bowed their heads. Now only the dad's mouth was moving. Even though Rex and Matilda couldn't hear what he was saying, by the look on their faces, it had to be good. Then just as suddenly as it had started, it stopped, and they all began to eat their meal.

That night before beginning to eat, Rex and Matilda smiled at each other. Then they took each other by the hands, closed their eyes, and bowed their heads. Noticing how quiet they were, their mom asked, "Now what are you two up to?" They just giggled as their dad smiled and shook his head.

The next day, Rex and Matilda headed straight for the park. They looked for Peter everywhere then decided to go to his house. Without warning, Peter came bounding out the front door. "See you later, Mom!" he called out as he ran toward the park. Rex was just about to run after him when Matilda said, "Rex, look!" There before them was the most amazing tree! Nothing like this grew in the desert by their home. Its branches were full of long leaves in the prettiest color green. It looked so soft!

Surprisingly, Matilda was the first one to climb up. Finally, Rex stopped staring and followed behind her. They bounced from branch to branch and climbed out to the very end of the leaves so they could just relax and sway in the breeze. Then off in the distance, they heard Peter laughing, so they ran off to find him.

That night before they fell asleep, Rex and Matilda decided that this tree would be their most favorite tree. After all, it was at the home of their favorite boy. It just seemed right.

As time passed, Rex and Matilda went about their days as usual. Wake up early, breakfast and chores, explore all day, and then finally dinner and a good night's sleep so they could do it all over again. With the love of their mom and dad, they were growing up strong and healthy.

One night at dinner, Rex and Matilda's dad said to them, "Your mother and I need to discuss something very important with you." They knew that when their dad talked liked this, it was going to be serious. "As you know," he continued, "the seasons are changing and it's that time of year again, when we must find our places to sleep until the warm weather returns." The whole family was paying attention as he continued. "In the past, your mom and I have picked a place for you, but we feel that you are more grown up now and should be able to choose for yourselves." Rex couldn't believe his ears! For a quick second, he could actually feel himself growing up. Then Rex enthusiastically focused on his dad again as he went on. "We trust you and know that you will find yourselves a safe place to rest. In the spring, when we awake, our family will meet back here." All the while their mom was looking at them with eyes full of love and pride. Rex and Matilda were so excited!

In bed that night, they talked and talked about just the right place. Finally, as if they both thought of it at the exact same time, Rex and Matilda exclaimed, "Peter's tree!" Happy that their very important decision was made, they closed their eyes and fell fast asleep.

Before the sun was in the sky the next morning, Rex and Matilda were waiting for breakfast. It must have been all that hard thinking the night before, because they woke up hungrier than they could ever remember. While they were munching away, their mom asked the question. "Well, have you decided on your place?" Eagerly shaking their heads, they began to describe the tree to her. "I remember seeing a tree like that when I was younger," their mom said. "It sounds like the perfect spot!" For the rest of the day, the family stayed close together. Their mom prepared the family's favorite foods so they could all fill up for their long sleep.

As night began to fall, everyone knew that the moment had come. In great detail, Rex and Matilda's mom and dad went over all the rules they needed to follow—especially the one about staying together and looking after one another. Then they kissed their children sweetly and hugged them for what seemed to be forever. Finally, staying very close to each other, the brother and sister hurried off to their special tree.

Rex and Matilda were a little nervous out on their own. They had never been this far from home this late before, and it seemed so very dark. Just then, an unexpected surprise appeared before them. All of the houses were covered in twinkling lights! As a matter of fact, it seemed that everything was covered in colored lights! The homes, the trees—everywhere they looked was sprinkled with color. Neither one of them had ever seen houses like these, and they wondered if this was how they always looked after the sun went down. All their nervousness just melted away as they took in the scene before them.

Then they saw their tree! It was even better than before. Somehow, the most beautiful big red flowers had bloomed on it overnight! They were more excited than ever about choosing this tree as their sleeping place for the winter!

With one more look around, Rex and Matilda smiled at each other and dug deep into the dirt. Snuggling up real close to each other, they fell fast asleep. They had no way of knowing that because of their choice, this was just the beginning of many more wonderful surprises in store for them.

Now the days were getting cooler and shorter. When the sun went down, the air was crisp and cold. For a while, Peter looked for his tiny friends in all their usual places. Even though he knew this was the time of year that they began to hibernate, he was still a little disappointed to think that he may not see them again for many months to come.

Finally, the day came when Peter knew that winter was here to stay. Every year at the same time, his mom would gather up any young plants she had and bring them indoors. She would always say out loud, "OK, my little ones—time to come in from the cold!" Peter loved how his mom talked to the plants like they really understood. This year, she looked at Peter and said, "I could sure use some muscles—this little guy has gotten heavy!" Unaware of the tiny stowaways, Peter and his mom carefully brought the palm in and placed it next to the fireplace. It fit right in with all the other Christmas decorations the family had placed around the hearth.

As Peter hung some sparkly ornaments on the palm, his excitement began to grow! This was his favorite time of the year. He loved Christmas the most and could hardly wait for all the festivities! Remembering his little friends one last time, he thought, "It really was too bad that they slept through this time of year."

Suddenly, Peter smelled something delicious coming from the kitchen. His mom was baking some of her favorite Christmas cookies! Peter waited all year for these yummy treats, and he ran into the kitchen for his first taste of the season. Any thoughts of Rex and Matilda drifted away––they were off somewhere, sleeping for the winter. Peter knew that there really wasn't any chance of seeing them again until the spring—or at least that was what he thought. Little did he know . . .

Rex stirred in the warm dirt. Before his eyes were even open, his senses were awakening. As he lazily lifted one eyelid, he thought to himself, *Could it be spring already?*

He felt like he had just fallen asleep. Why did the earth seem so warm? Slowly he stretched and then searched for Matilda. She was curled up in a little ball right behind him. He gently nudged his sister and whispered, "Wake up, sleepyhead." Matilda grumbled and turned over. Rex began to dig upward.

Never before had he been this shocked in his whole life! Where were they? This was not outside Peter's house! He didn't recognize a single thing he saw. He didn't even notice Matilda surfacing, but her loud shriek made him jump straight up! Quickly he covered her mouth—they needed to be quiet until they figured out what had happened while they were sleeping. Rex held Matilda close and whispered, "Stay quiet!" Cautiously they took a few steps forward. Suddenly, they heard an unfamiliar voice off in the distance. It was a deep, strong voice, and

Rex and Matilda timidly hid behind a palm leaf. Slowly, very slowly, Rex peeked out and searched the room. On the far side of the room was a man—Peter's dad. Rex had never heard Peter's dad speak before. Now that he knew who it was, he relaxed a little and let his curiosity take over. What he saw next made his tiny heart skip a beat—it was Peter! Yes, there he was, sitting right next to his dad. Somehow, they had ended up inside of Peter's house! As Rex and Matilda relaxed to the soothing sound of this new voice, they looked around and took in the cozy sights before them. It was then that they realized something else as well—it wasn't springtime yet, and they were about to see things that their kind could only dream of.

Rex focused his eyes across the room. Peter and his dad were snuggled up close to each other. Between them was a large book with many pages. Off in the distance from somewhere they couldn't see, Rex and Matilda heard the familiar voice of Peter's mom. She was lightly humming the prettiest song they had ever heard. Softly, the words from Peter's dad drifted across the room. From what Rex could hear, he was telling Peter a story of a very special baby that came into the world. Rex heard Peter's dad say that this baby was born in the desert, and he was sent to be the King of kings. Instantly, Rex sharpened his attention and focused in on the story—after all, he was also a king born in the desert.

"Tell me again, Daddy," Peter said. Now the words from Peter's dad were as clear as a bell.

"Mary, the baby's mother was promised to be married to Joseph, but before they came together, she was found to be with child through the Holy Spirit," he said peacefully.

"An angel of the Lord appeared to Joseph in a dream and told him that Mary would give birth to a son, and that he should be given the name Jesus, because through his love he would save all his people." Peter looked up at his father and asked, "The true Light of the world would show the people the way, Daddy?" Peter's dad put his arm around his boy. "Yes, son," he gently continued. "Joseph went on to Bethlehem with Mary. While they were there, the time came for the baby to be born. After the baby Jesus came into the world, Mary wrapped him in cloths and placed him in a manger because there was no room for them at the inn."

Peter's eyes were now closed, but Rex knew he wasn't sleeping. Rex also closed his eyes so that he too could try to imagine the story being told. Peter's father went on, "The shepherds were keeping watch over their flocks at night when an angel appeared to them and the glory of the Lord shone all around them. The angel told them 'Do not be afraid, I bring you good news of great joy that will be for all people. Today a Savior has been born to you. He is Christ, the Lord. Glory to God in the highest, and peace on earth.' The shepherds hurried off to Bethlehem and found Mary, Joseph, and the baby, who was lying in the manger. After seeing him, the shepherds spread the word told to them by the angels. And all who heard of the wondrous event were amazed at what the shepherds said to them."

Peter's mother came into the room now and sat down next to her son. She smiled at her boy and added, "But Mary, mother of the baby Jesus, treasured up all these things and pondered them in her heart." Peter finished by softly adding, "And this was the day that God showed the world how much He loves us." Peter's father gently closed the book and gave his son a loving hug. Never before had Rex ever seen his boy so happy and content. There quietly tucked away in the palm tree, Rex felt very happy too.

Out of nowhere, Matilda tackled Rex so hard that they both almost fell from the tree. Standing over him, she could hardly contain her excitement. "Wait until you see what I've found!" She dashed away again and Rex followed, still thinking of the beautiful story that Peter's family had just shared with him.

As he turned the corner, Rex's mouth began to water as his belly growled. He saw Matilda straight ahead of him. Wonderful smells were all around as he raced up behind her. When he reached the top of the table, his eyes opened wide. Never before had he ever seen so many delicious-looking foods in one place! Again Matilda disappeared, but luckily Rex found her tiny little footprints. He followed them across the table, occasionally stopping to lick the sticky powder off his fingers or take a nibble from a tasty treat.

"Isn't this delightful!" Matilda shouted. Once again, his little sister made him jump, only this time Rex landed right in a big bowl of brightly colored sugar-coated gumdrops! Matilda laughed and laughed, while Rex tried to pull himself up out of the bowl. Rex couldn't help but laugh himself. "What have you been eating, sis?" he asked.

"What haven't I been eating is more like it!" Matilda giggled. "I've munched on everything!" she said proudly. Rex grabbed a cookie and then split it to share with his sister. They sat for a moment, looking over the different colored candies in each cookie, carefully making sure to sample each one.

Looking at his sister, Rex asked, "Did you hear any of the story Peter's father was telling?" Matilda looked up from her cookie. "Just something about a baby being born in the desert," she answered. "We've heard stories like that before, so I decided to explore, and that's when I found all this wonderful stuff!" Rex put his treat down and stood up. "Oh no, Matilda," he said, "we've never heard a story like this one!" Rex began to enthusiastically repeat the story the best he could to his sister. She gave him her complete attention. While she was listening, Matilda realized something. Never before had she ever seen her brother so excited about a story, unless it was about himself. Something was different about Rex's face and as Matilda watched her brother, she was very happy for him. "*This baby Jesus must be someone very special indeed*," she thought. Rex finished telling the story just in time. The voices of Peter and his family could be heard again, so Rex and Matilda hurried down from the table.

Peter's family wasn't sitting together in the room with the palm tree anymore, and Rex and Matilda could hear their voices fading away. As they made their way down the hallway, they saw Peter, his mom, and his dad. "Good night, Daddy," they heard Peter say. Then he gave his dad a big hug and disappeared out of sight with his mother. From far off in the distance, Rex and Matilda heard their boy giggle softly while his mom was tucking him in. Finally, they heard the shuffle of feet above them, and then all was quiet in the house. They were just about to follow when something caught their attention.

From an open door, there came a soft glow. It was completely quiet now, and it seemed almost magical the way the many colors were dancing in the silence. Rex and Matilda inched their way toward the entrance of the room. As they peeked around the door, their eyes widened with glee! In the middle of the room was a huge tree covered with hundreds of lights! With one quick glance, they were sure of one thing—there was more fun in this room than they could ever imagine!

Rex and Matilda didn't know where to start. They ran to the tree and played hide and seek among the many cheerfully wrapped presents. Then they raced from one end to the other in long tunnels made of shiny paper. Rex climbed up on a branch and dove right into a big box of brightly colored bows. They were soft and bouncy, so he called his sister over for a try. Matilda shrieked with joy as she jumped over and over again.

Suddenly, they saw tiny tracks in front of them. With their noses to the ground, they slowly circled the tree. Rex bumped his head on the train, then looked up and climbed aboard. Matilda quickly climbed up and settled into the car behind him. "What is this thing, Rex?" He looked around at all the little buttons in front of him. "I don't know sis," he said as he pushed down on one. The train jumped forward as Rex and Matilda held on tightly! Rex pushed another button, and a whistle blew! He pushed still another, and a tiny stream of smoke rose from the train! "This is wonderful!" Matilda shouted. "Make the whistle sound again!" Rex gave his sister a big grin as they went round and round the tree. "This is fantastic!" he said. "Look how fast we're going, and we're not even running!" Finally, after riding for what seemed to be forever, Rex began pushing more buttons. The train slowly came to a stop, and Rex and Matilda tumbled to the floor.

As they were gazing up at the tree, they began to notice all the different hanging ornaments. "I have an idea," Matilda said. "Let's start at the bottom and look at each one." Rex agreed, and they began to explore. "Look at this, Matilda!" She ran to her brother and found him in front of a huge shiny red ball. She could see his reflection in the ball as he made funny faces at himself. "You are so silly!" she laughed, and then she joined right in with him. When they finished making funny faces, they went on to the other ornaments, one by one. Slowly, they made their way to the top of the tree. At the very top was a big, bright star.

While Matilda was climbing to the very top of it, something down below caught Rex's eye. He could see a tiny glowing light. It was different from all the other lights in the room, and Rex wanted to get closer.

He was very excited as he scurried down the tree. He crossed the room to the place where he had seen the light. As he climbed up the leg of the table, the glow became brighter. Nothing he had done or seen this night had prepared him for what was before him. His heart skipped a beat as his eyes fell on the tiniest little people he had ever seen. The most curious feeling came over him—these people were the same size as he was, yet for some reason, he had never felt so small.

At once, he remembered the story of the baby Jesus as his heart skipped another beat! He searched the faces of the tiny people and began to recognize them. There were the shepherds with their sheep! "*Who were these three other men gathered nearby?*" he wondered. Then, right in the middle, he saw the smiling faces of Joseph and Mary! Joseph was standing over the light, while Mary was on her knees beside it.

Rex slowly made his way to the light and looked in. A tiny baby was lying peacefully with light shining all around him. He had the most beautiful look of love on his face, and Rex knew that this was the baby Jesus! As Rex gazed in wonder at the baby, a feeling of calm came over him. Rex, king of the desert, humbly knew that he was standing before the Light of the world. Never before had he felt more special than at this moment, but the funny thing was, it wasn't for all the old reasons. He now knew that he was so very special because the King of kings loved him.

Rex lay peacefully looking in on the baby. He never even noticed Matilda quietly coming up behind him. "Rex?" she whispered. He slowly lifted his head and whispered back. "Come see." As Matilda came closer, her little foot stepped on a small button and music began to play. They both instantly recognized the song.

"Silent Night, Holy Night ♪"

It was the song that Peter's mother had been humming earlier. It was the song about the night the baby Jesus was born. Matilda snuggled next to her brother and peeked in at the baby. "This is him, Matilda—the baby Jesus from the story." Matilda's heart felt like it was going to burst with joy as she gazed at him. "He loves me, Matilda, and He loves you too." They lay there with all the other animals, welcoming the new baby into the world as the soft music played. Never before had Rex and Matilda felt such amazing love, and with thoughts of His love still lingering in their hearts, they slowly drifted off into the most peaceful sleep they had ever known.

The sun was up, and it was Christmas morning! Peter flew down the stairs as fast as he could. He couldn't wait to see what kind of surprises were under the tree, but he knew where he wanted to stop first. He went straight to the Nativity to say Happy Birthday to Jesus and thank Him for the best gift of all – His Love.

Peter gasped with surprise as he saw the two tiny creatures curled up next to the manger. "How did you two get here?" he whispered.

Rex and Matilda didn't even know that their boy was standing over them. Peter smiled and thought to himself *"What a wonderful gift! An unexpected visit from two of my favorite friends who also wanted to be close to Jesus at Christmas!"*

Peter knew his little friends couldn't stay sleeping there, but he knew it was too cold to put them outside. In a flash, Peter had an idea that made his face light up. "*The palm tree by the fireplace!*" he thought. Gently, he lifted Rex and Matilda up and brought them to the palm. He dug a hold deep in the dirt, and carefully placed them inside. So exhausted from the adventures of the previous night, they never even felt their boy gently push the dirt back over them like a comfy blanket. Peter looked at the neat little space with pride, completely pleased with himself that he had come up with such a good solution to keep his friends safe and warm for the winter.

Peter's mom and dad were coming down the stairs now, calling out to him. "Merry Christmas, Peter! Where's our guy?" Peter smiled, thinking how blessed he was, and called out cheerfully, "Here I am!" Then he ran off to join his parents, jumping into their arms for his share of Christmas morning hugs and kisses.

As the sounds of Christmas began to fill their home, Peter and his family savored the day with all the joys and blessings that came with it.

Unaware of their festivities, Peter's tiny friends slumbered peacefully. They were fast asleep, dreaming of the baby Jesus.

# About the Author

Jodi was born and raised in New York and moved to Arizona with her family in the mid-1990s. Pierre is a Lebanese-born Christian, who became a US citizen in the mid-1980s. He also moved to the Prescott area, where he served Christ through his involvement with local churches. In 2001, the two met under very challenging times, and it was here that their lives would change forever.

The concept of this book had been with Jodi since her arrival in the Southwest years before, but it wasn't until she became a Christian that she understood the purpose it would come to serve. Being a mother, it was initially meant to fill a gap for her children where snowmen and sleds were no longer typical at this time of year. But that changed after she herself was humbled by God's perfect gift.

After over fifteen years of dedicated friendship, the story still holds the same joy for these friends as when it was first conceived. Their hope is that it brings this same joy to your family as well.

Printed in the USA
CPSIA information can be obtained
at www.ICGtesting.com
JSHW040028110923
47556JS00001B/2